Hero School

Based on the episode
"Looking After Gekko"

Ready-to-Read

Simon Spotlight
New York   London   Toronto   Sydney   New Delhi

SIMON SPOTLIGHT
An imprint of Simon & Schuster Children's Publishing Division
1230 Avenue of the Americas, New York, New York 10020
This Simon Spotlight edition July 2017
Adapted by Tina Gallo from the series PJ Masks
All rights reserved, including the right of reproduction in whole or in part in any form.
SIMON SPOTLIGHT, READY-TO-READ, and colophon are registered trademarks of
Simon & Schuster, Inc.
For information about special discounts for bulk purchases, please contact
Simon & Schuster Special Sales at 1-866-506-1949 or business@simonandschuster.com.
Manufactured in the United States of America 0418 LAK
10 9 8 7 6 5 4 3 2
ISBN 978-1-4814-9176-1 (hc)
ISBN 978-1-4814-9175-4 (pbk)
ISBN 978-1-4814-9177-8 (eBook)

Greg is excited to take a
book home from school.

Greg reaches for a book.

It is too high.

Greg falls.

Connor and Amaya get
the book for Greg.
They walk to the
school bus.

Oh no! The school bus
is missing!
This looks like a job for
the PJ Masks!

Amaya becomes Owlette!

Greg becomes

Gekko!

Connor becomes
Catboy!

They are the PJ Masks!

Gekko wants to drive.

The PJ Masks see the
school bus! They chase it.

The Gekko-Mobile

is too slow.

The bus gets away.

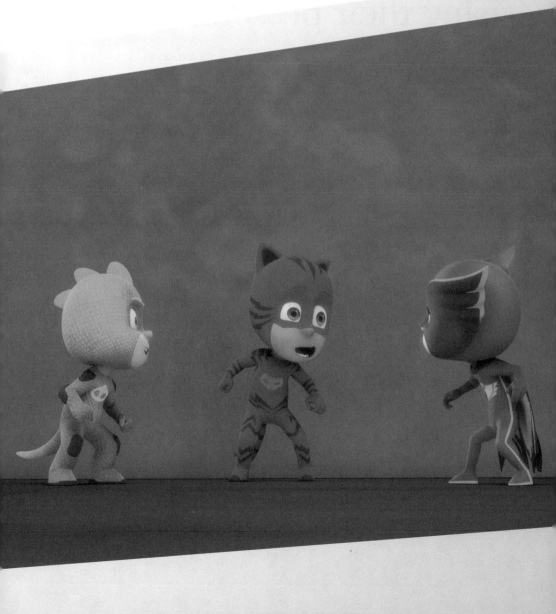

"Cat Ears!" says Catboy.

"Owl Eyes!" says Owlette.

They find the bus
using their powers.

The bus is in the town square! Gekko wants to be the hero.

Gekko drives to
the town square.
Night Ninja has the bus!

The Ninjalinos are
painting the bus blue.
"Give back the bus,"
Gekko says.

"No! The bus will be
my super-car!"
Night Ninja says.

Night Ninja throws
Sticky-Splats.
Gekko is in trouble!

Owlette and Catboy arrive.
"We will help, Gekko!"
they say.

Gekko does not want help.

Night Ninja throws Sticky-Splats at Catboy.

Owlette gets tangled.

"Only I can stop
Night Ninja now!"
Gekko says.

"Super Gekko Muscles!"

Gekko says.

He takes the bus

from Night Ninja.

But Night Ninja steals
the Gekko-Mobile!
Gekko calls for help.

Owlette gets free.

Then she helps Catboy.

Together they help Gekko.

The PJ Masks toss
Night Ninja out of the
Gekko-Mobile.

"You will not beat me
next time!"
Night Ninja says.

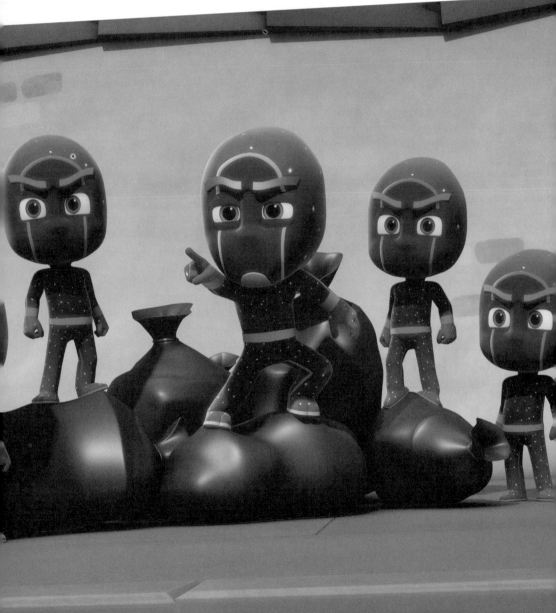

"When we help each other, we cannot be beat!"

Gekko says.

The heroes return the bus to school!

Gekko learned that even heroes need help sometimes. Hooray for the PJ Masks!